To my Eggun, for always leading the way.
To Mami and Papi for loving me as best they could and for sharing me with
Mamá and Papá. I don't know how you did it but I'm glad you did.
To all my siblings, blood-related and love-bonded, for caring for me in such
a way that left no room for me to ever doubt whether I was loved or not.
And to Elena, who inspires me to be a better mami and woman every day.
Don't ever stop speaking your truth, my love. From here to the sun and
back, until the ancestors no longer stand by our side.
—S. R.

For all we are and can be
—B. M.

SIMON & SCHUSTER BOOKS FOR YOUNG READERS
An imprint of Simon & Schuster Children's Publishing Division
1230 Avenue of the Americas, New York, New York 10020
Text copyright © 2020 by Sili Recio
Illustrations copyright © 2020 by Brianna McCarthy
SIMON & SCHUSTER BOOKS FOR YOUNG READERS is a trademark of Simon & Schuster, Inc.
For information about special discounts for bulk purchases, please contact Simon & Schuster Special
Sales at 1-866-506-1949 or business@simonandschuster.com.
The Simon & Schuster Speakers Bureau can bring authors to your live event. For more information
or to book an event, contact the Simon & Schuster Speakers Bureau at 1-866-248-3049 or visit our
website at www.simonspeakers.com.
Book design by Lizzy Bromley
The text for this book was set in Harman Elegant.
The illustrations for this book were rendered in mixed media.
Manufactured in China · 1120 SCP
2 4 6 8 10 9 7 5 3
Library of Congress Cataloging-in-Publication Data
Names: Recio, Sili, author. | McCarthy, Brianna, illustrator.
Title: If Dominican were a color / Sili Recio ; illustrated by Brianna McCarthy.
Description: First edition. | New York : Simon & Schuster Books for Young Readers, [2020] | Audience:
Ages 4–8. | Audience: Grades K-1. | Summary: Illustrations and easy-to-read text portray the Dominican
Republic in all of its hues, from the cinnamon in cocoa to the blue black seen only in dreams.
Identifiers: LCCN 2019029355 (print) | LCCN 2019029356 (eBook) |
ISBN 9781534461796 (hardcover) | ISBN 9781534461802 (eBook)
Subjects: LCSH: Dominican Republic–Fiction. | CYAC: Dominican Republic–Fiction.
Classification: LCC PZ7.1.R3979 If 2020 (print) | LCC PZ7.1.R3979 (eBook) | DDC [E]–dc23
LC record available at https://lccn.loc.gov/2019029355
LC eBook record available at https://lccn.loc.gov/2019029356

IF DOMINICAN WERE A COLOR

WERE A COLOR

Written by Sili Recio

Illustrated by Brianna McCarthy

A DENENE MILLNER BOOK

Simon & Schuster Books for Young Readers

New York   London   Toronto   Sydney   New Delhi

IF DOMINICAN WERE A COLOR...

it would be the sunset in the sky,
blazing red and burning bright.

The shade of cinnamon in your cocoa,

the drums beating so fast, they drive you loco.

My grandma's mahogany skin,
honey brown eyes.
My other grandma's yellow
tint, just like mine.

If Dominican were a color . . .

it would be the shades of
orange in the sunrise's hue,

the Haitian black on
my Dominican back.

The deep green tints that
carry the palm tree shades,
the memories in your head
that never fade.

The neutral browns
that color our lips,
the *café con leche*
that everyone sips.

If Dominican were a color . . .
it'd be merengue hips
swaying when I walk,

the chatter of
neighbors, strutting
as they talk.

It'd be the way my words
shape in my mouth,
the color they might not
know in the South.

It would be the hopscotch from my *niñez*,
and counting jacks from one to *diez*.

It'd be the curls and kinks
that blend my hair,
the color of charcoal
mixed with the sun's glare.

If Dominican were a color . . .
it'd be the roar of the ocean in the deep of night,
with the moon beaming down rays of sheer delight.

It'd be the *maíz* coming up *amarillo* with green.

It'd be the blue black you only see in a dream.

There wouldn't be a palette that could hold it all.
It's the seasons put together—
summer, winter, spring, and fall.

AUTHOR'S NOTE

When my mother and I left the Dominican Republic to live with my black, Spanish-speaking father in New York City, he seared these words into my head: "You're black, and don't you forget it." It was an easy demand for me to meet; as a little girl in Dominican Republic, my world was filled with love—and melanin. *Mis padres de crianza*, loosely translated to "the parents that helped raise me," were a ribbon of different shades of brown, and they showered me with love and self-love that made me appreciate the skin I'm in.

Mamá and I are both "java," a term used on the island to describe a person with light skin and black features. Papá and my two sisters are as dark as the chocolate Embajador they sell in the stores. We have curly hair and the more we played in the sun, the more our brown stood out. We thought our colors were beautiful.

Still, for all the love that our little family unit shared during those slow summer days, some memories are tarnished by how others tried to shape blackness in my eyes. To them, looking black instead of like family members who looked white was worthy of insults. What they didn't understand was that neither racism nor colorism could ever change the beauty I saw in my features—how I saw myself.

So many people back on the island have yet to embrace this simple truth—my truth: that black is beautiful. And that's a shame considering how many dark-skinned Dominicans and other dark-skinned citizens of Spanish-speaking countries exist. Though many ships landed in the United States during the transatlantic slave trade, they made up only a small percentage compared to the ships that dropped enslaved Africans in the Caribbean and Central and South America. In the Dominican Republic specifically, it is estimated that 73 percent of the population is racially mixed, meaning that blackness literally colors our country in more ways than most care to admit.

This book is for the little boys and girls who were never nourished with the balm of truth—those who may have felt as if they did not belong because of their dark complexions or curly hair texture or the width of their noses. This is for those who've been told they are ugly simply because they wear their African ancestors' beauty on their faces and in their hair. This is for little black boys and girls who have yet to step into their power and magic because society leans on its own biases to tell them they are not worthy. This book is for those who proudly check that "black" box on the census because they know exactly who they are and for those, too, who are just figuring it out, whether they are age four or age forty.

The island is full of color, as is the world. I celebrate it. And you. Because you're black and I don't want you to forget it.